DRAGON THIEF SERIES

<u>SEASON ONE</u>
Dragon Thief
The Chicago Job
The Poisons Book Job
The Vault Job
The Femme Fatale Job
The Scavenger Job

<u>SEASON TWO</u>
The Crown of Kingship Job
The Green Scroll Job
The Payback Job

DRAGON THIEF
A DRAGON THIEF STORY

DRAGON THIEF
BOOK ONE

KAT SIMONS

T&D PUBLISHING

DRAGON THIEF

To my own tall man. Love you, sweetie.
And to my heroes in training…
Who are making fine work of that training.

ONE

Who steals a dragon?

Myra had stolen a lot of things in her life. Jewels. Magic objects. Money. But a dragon?

Even she wasn't that brazen.

Yet, here she was, breaking into a high security building the middle of downtown Manhattan because someone else had the stupid idea to *steal* a dragon shifter. Just… Myra wasn't even sure what to call it. Hutzpah. But that felt too complimentary. Gall felt too weak. Idiocy maybe? Idiocy seemed like a good word.

She felt like a bit of an idiot, too, for allowing herself to get roped into this.

But she supposed this was what you got when you messed with a dragon king.

She crept silently from the closet where she'd used an untraceable, and disposable, laptop to hack into the building's security system and disable the motion sensors along the routes she needed. She'd also set the security cameras on a loop so they wouldn't record her activity. The guards outside her destination were going to be a little trickier, but according to the schedule she'd found in the security records, they'd be changing in less than ten minutes which gave her a tiny window of opportunity.

She just had to get into the locked room. She'd be getting back out again through a route that bypassed those guards.

If all went to plan, she'd get in, get the dragon king's son, and get out again without anyone being the wiser. His kidnappers would walk in to discover an empty room, and it would take them a week to figure out how it had all happened.

But that was if all went to plan.

Unfortunately, in Myra's experience, things rarely went to plan.

She waited in a corridor where she could see the guards outside her destination, but hear the changing guard coming in. There would be a moment, when they stood outside the antechamber exchanging codes and information. Not long. Forty-five seconds maybe. But that should give her enough time to pick the lock and get inside.

The sounds of the approaching guards had her gut tightening and a small smile played across her mouth. She did love her job. Even the anxiety was a rush.

Using a little touch of magic to disguise herself—hiding her scent and any visual cues that might give her away to people used to working with shapeshifters—she waited for the guards inside the antechamber to step out and speak with the incoming guards. All of them were large, three men, one woman, every single one dressed in a pants suit, except one of the men who wore a kilt. She admired the fashion sense in what would otherwise be a pretty matched set of individuals.

She snuck across the hall behind them, relying on her magical screening spell to keep herself hidden, then paused just inside the antechamber and listened. No alerts. No one had heard her.

So far so good.

Hurrying to the locked door, she pulled her lockpicks out from inside her multi-pocket vest and knelt down. It wasn't a complicated lock. Mostly there for show. What they had inside couldn't be contained with an ordinary door lock.

She finessed it in fourteen seconds, without even having to use a magical push, and slid inside, quietly closing the door behind her. She relocked the door from inside, just in case someone thought to test it. Then she held perfectly still, her ear to the door, listening as the new guards settled into place with a minimum of conversation.

When no one sounded an alarm, she took a deep breath and turned to face the room. Smiling. One step down. Now the important part.

The room was a large, bare, concrete box. The floor, the walls, even the ceiling just bare concrete. No paint or decoration. No rugs or carpets. No wood. Nothing that would easily burn. There were no windows either, even though the room was located on an outside corner of the high-rise.

The door she'd come through was "wood" on the outside, but inside it was obviously solid steel. From this side, it looked like a vault door. A vault door with a shitty and useless lock, but still pretty solid.

It wasn't the lock that was keeping the occupant inside the bare concrete room, though.

No. That was the chains.

Because the lights in the room were very low, barely above nightlight for visibility purposes, she heard the chains before she saw them. The dragon king had warned her those would be there. She came prepared. Still, hearing the chink chink against the concrete floor gave her a little shiver. Poor kid.

She didn't dare speak until she got closer, because while the guards looked like ordinary humans who relied on more mundane forms of security, they were guards used to working with shifters and might well be shifters themselves. She didn't dare tempt their hearing. She was only confident they wouldn't pick up her scent because she'd disguised that to open the door.

They weren't the only ones used to working around shifters.

She wasn't one herself. Just a garden variety thief. With the right kind of magic to make that job infinitely more fun. But when you went in to steal a certain grade of collectibles, it did put you in the way of shifters as well as other members of the magical community.

Myra didn't mind. She liked the challenge.

Though, as she crept closer to the hunched form opposite the door, huddled under what looked like a thick blanket, she decided dealing with dragons who could breathe fire and crisp her in under a second was not the kind of challenge she wanted to repeat in the future if she could at all help it.

She stared at that hunched form under the blanket as she approached carefully, wondering if the kid was okay since he wasn't moving. She had no idea what to expect from the dragon king's son. She hadn't even been shown a picture. Something something, no pictures of royal family taken, something something. Hadn't made sense to her, but whatever. The dragons could do as they liked. She was just told the stolen shifter was the king's son. And he wasn't being held for ransom or anything normal like that. Apparently, there was some other nefarious plot afoot. Which the king had also not seen fit to explain to her.

And that was fine, too. She didn't need to know what the kidnappers had in mind for the king's son. She just needed to know where he was so she could get him out. Steal him back, so to speak. Then she got the dragon king off her back for their little misunderstanding, and all would be right in Myra's world. She could go back to stealing what she wanted to steal.

The hunched form remained motionless as she neared. She was pretty sure the little guy would know she was here by now, because even though her spell to confuse shifter senses was still in place, she suspected a dragon shifter, even a young one, would just *feel* someone in the room with them.

Not taking that into account was what had gotten her into trouble with the dragon king.

But the closer she got to the king's son, the more she worried. Was he okay? The king said he was young, but hadn't said how young, and her imagination conjured images of a shivering, shaking, terrified child trying not to show just how scared he was as he huddled underneath the blanket.

When she was close enough to whisper without being easily overheard by the guards, she murmured, "Hey, it's okay. I'm here to get you out. You don't have to be scared of me. I'm a friend of your dad's. I'll have you out of here and back to him soon."

The hunched form finally moved a little, so Myra stilled, giving the boy time to adjust to her. She didn't want him to accidentally fry her with a blast of fire he couldn't control because of fear.

But as she watched, the hunched form got larger and larger. And now she worried he was trying to shift inside this concrete room on the fortieth floor of a high-rise building.

That would be really really bad.

"Listen, don't shift. Okay. There's not enough room." There were innocent people in this building as well as the thieves. She did not want the place brought down by a youngling dragon shifting and destroying half the building in the process.

The form unhunched completely as a very deep voice said, "I'm not an idiot and neither are they. I can't shift, even if I was stupid enough to do it."

Myra blinked a few times. That voice sounded very…adult for a kid.

She blinked a few more times as the hunched form tossed off the blanket that had been covering him.

Uh.

That was no youngling kid.

Two

The fully grown adult man sitting on the concrete floor was a revelation to Myra, having been under the impression she was here to rescue a child. And wasn't that the last time she took a dragon king's phrasing at face value.

"Youngling my ass," she muttered as she approached the man. "Do not fry me. Your father did send me."

"Why you?"

"Because I'm an excellent thief," she murmured as she got close enough to inspect the chains.

And close enough to get a good look at the king's son.

He wasn't what she might call ordinarily

handsome. The messy dark hair and blue eyes were pretty conventionally attractive, she supposed. But his features were too broad, and heavy, and maybe a little too sharp. There was a scar across his jaw, under beard scruff. And another across his forehead.

He looked a little worse for wear, and not just because his button-down shirt and dress pants were rumpled. He looked like he'd been going a few rounds in the shifter fight club.

No, not conventionally handsome, like his kingly father. Definitely not pretty.

But all of it together—his broad face and messy hair and scars—really…worked for him. He didn't need ordinary handsome. He had something more, something compelling that was…

Frankly, a little distracting.

She couldn't afford to be distracted right now. Breaking magic binding chains took a very special sort of concentration. And they only had a small window of time to make this work.

"I've had my fill of thieves over the last few days," the dragon muttered. There was a rawness to his voice, like he hadn't had anything to drink recently.

"You'll be rid of me soon enough," she said.

She pulled a bottle of water from one of the myriad pockets in her vest and handed it to him.

He stared at the bottle for a long moment.

She waved it at him and held his gaze. "Just water. No spells. I'm a thief, not a wizard. My magic doesn't do poison or anything like that."

"What does your magic do?" he asked as he took the bottle.

She smiled a little as she looked down at the cuffs on his ankles and the one on his wrist. "Makes locks into puzzle toys," she murmured.

The cuffs keeping a fully grown dragon shifter captive weren't things to be taken lightly, of course. These were made from some of the best quality steel she'd ever seen, infused with a copper alloy that held the magic, which raced over the surface of the cuffs in a swirl of purplish-blue light. The cuffs were attached to chains with links as thick as her forearms, and those were bolted to the floor by more thick, fused metal with lines of magic swirling through it.

So, not easy. But also, not outside her skill set.

A little rush of adrenaline-fueled excitement moved through her as she pulled out her lockpick case again.

"Why can't I smell you?" the man asked.

"Spell. Lot of shifters around." She had most of her attention on the cuffs, but his voice sounded less raw so she assumed he was drinking the water she'd given him.

"But you're not a wizard?"

"No wizard magic. Just thief magic." She grinned at him. "Don't worry. I'm a good thief."

"Is that why my father sent you?"

She winced inwardly. "Mostly."

"What does mostly mean?"

"Shh. I have to concentrate." She returned her attention to the cuffs, and her leather lockpick satchel as she selected her tools.

"No one shushes me."

"Maybe they should. You're not very good at it." She pulled out two long, thin picks, then set her fingers against the ankle cuff. Shook her head. Replaced the two picks and pulled out another two. Yes, those would do.

"I'm a king's son and a dragon shifter. No one shushes me."

She let out a deep, impatient breath and met his gaze again. "Listen, do you want out of here or not?"

"I want out of here."

"Then hush. I have to focus. And we only have so much time."

His eyes narrowed, but he didn't speak again.

"Finally," she muttered. Then she set to work on the locks.

Not her best time. The ankle cuffs took a little more finessing than she'd hoped and there was a moment there when she actually worried a little. But still, in under ten minutes she had him completely free and was setting the magic infused cuffs gently aside.

"Don't burn anything, and don't shift," she said as the man stretched his legs out and gave his body a big shake.

"I'm not an idiot," he said, glaring at her.

"Just have to make sure. Dragons…" She waved her hand in the air and hoped that explained everything.

From the way his gaze narrowed further, she assumed it hadn't. Or he was just unhappy with the explanation.

Either way, they didn't have time for her to sort through his grumpy facial expression. "Can you stand? Do you need help?"

She had no idea how long he'd been chained in place, and the chains weren't long enough to have allowed for a wide range of movement. He'd been taken a week ago. If he'd been chained in this spot for all that time, he would probably be pretty sore and stiff.

"I can stand," he said, giving her a condescending look.

She snorted and shook her head. "Lot of

smugness for someone who went and got themselves stolen."

She stood back while he climbed to his feet, using the wall behind him to push upward. She collected his empty water bottle from the floor so he wouldn't have to bend down again, and slid the crumpled plastic into one of her inner pockets for later recycling.

His full height was something to behold. She wasn't what one might call tall. In fact, she had to stretch to reach medium. He, on the other hand, was… Well, tall was an understatement.

And that was going to complicate things.

She scowled. Glanced back at the door. No one seemed to have noticed them yet, which was good. But her escape plan had just taken a hit.

"Your dad should have warned me you weren't a kid," she muttered under her breath.

"He implied I was a child?"

"He called you a youngling." She faced him again, moving close enough to make sure they could speak quietly. He wasn't as stinky as she'd have expected after being held captive for a week in a concrete room. Little ripe, but not the sort of pungent sweat and fear stench she'd have expected. "Failed to give me your name, too. Lot of 'my son' but not a lot of name usage. What's your name?"

His expression was hard to read when he stood so much taller than her. How had he hunched in on himself enough to look like a kid when she'd walked in? Must be a lighting thing. And no that wasn't a flutter in her stomach because she adored tall men. That was…nerves. Just nerves.

"Christopher," he said, his voice deep.

Did he sound irritated? She thought he sounded irritated. But she didn't have time to deal with his irritation. "Listen, Chris—"

"Christopher. I don't like Chris."

"Fine. Christopher. My plan for getting out of here was predicated on the fact that you were… well, small. And since you are not small, things are going to get a little cramped. Are you claustrophobic?"

He shook his head. "But if you're thinking we can exit through the air ducts, they have motion sensors and alarms in those. It's not a viable option."

"Are you the thief here? No. I'm the thief. Trust me. I have that part covered." Questioning her bona fides. How rude. "And we only need the air ducts for a short section. Can you squish yourself up enough to do this? I don't have a plan for going back through that door without it bringing all the security in the building down on us. And that would be bad."

More than bad. It would be suicidal. The kidnappers knew how to contain a dragon or they wouldn't have gotten Christopher here. They'd know how to stop him trying to escape in an obvious way. The whole reason *she* was here was to sneak him out without anyone knowing until it was too late. So front door with the handy guards who would raise an alarm was not an option.

"I can manage." He didn't sound particularly confident, but he wasn't arguing with her either.

Good. She hated when the loot argued with her.

"You good to go now?" she asked. "All the blood returned to all the various body parts?" For reasons she refused to acknowledge, mentioning his body parts and blood flow made her stomach flutter again. Weird.

"I'm fine. I can manage."

"Groovy. Let's go."

If he'd been the child she was expecting, she'd have taken his hand. But since he wasn't a child and there was all this stomach fluttering stuff going on—nerves, just nerves about the plan getting complicated—she motioned him to follow her instead.

And tried to ignore the feel of all that muscle and heat just at her back.

THREE

The air duct was located high on the wall, near the ceiling. And of course, the screen wasn't just a simple, easily removeable screen. It was thicker metal than the usual vents, and it was locked into place. But it hadn't been massively reinforced with complicated locks and stuff either. After all, there were supposed to be motion sensors in the ducts. Why waste too much energy on an impenetrable screen?

The duct's location was a little tricky since Myra couldn't bring a regular ladder with her. The room had high ceilings, not outrageously high, but high enough she couldn't just jump up and touch the screen.

Because she'd assumed she was stealing back someone child-sized who wouldn't be able to just reach up and boost themselves into the vent, she had brought a foldable ladder she could hook into the duct once she had the screen off. She glanced at Christopher. Her ladder would not take his weight. But since he was tall enough—and she presumed strong enough by the looks of him—to boost himself up to the air duct, she figured they were still okay.

For her part, she just needed some wall climbing sticky pods. Like the kinds of thing used at rock climbing centers to simulate hand and foot holds along climbing walls, her pods did a similar thing, giving her hand and foot holds for scaling sheer surfaces. Her pods weren't bolted into anything of course, she just slapped them onto the wall. But since they were reinforced with a little magic, she didn't need the bolts.

The first pods went onto the wall just above her head level with one for a toe hold at her waist. She set an additional three pods as she needed them while she climbed, pulling them from another convenient vest pocket. She loved her vest pockets. There were so many of them. And they held so much. She wasn't sure how she'd managed to do stealing before she'd gotten this vest.

Once she reached the screen, she had it removed in short order, a few handy twists of her lockpicks to deal with the basic lock. With one hand holding a sticky pod, she hefted the heavy screen down the wall with her other hand.

"Take this," she grunted. "Gentle on the floor."

Christopher didn't argue with her or comment, just took the screen like it was a piece of paper and set it against the wall a foot away. She supposed that was better than if he'd been a kid. If he'd been a kid, she'd have had to climb back down the wall one handed to set the screen aside. It wasn't a long climb of course—the room wasn't that tall—but this did save a step.

"Can you climb using the hand and toe holds?" she asked. "Or can you just boost yourself up?" He didn't really have to stretch much to reach the air duct. His height really was pretty impressive.

"I'll follow," he said.

From this angle, looking more down at him than up, she could sort of see him better but that didn't help her read his expression any easier. Heavy eyebrows pulled down over his blue eyes, which were pretty arresting when she got a good look at them. His mouth was set in a line. His muscles were tight. And he kept glancing at the door.

But whether he was scared, irritated, bored, or angry, she couldn't tell.

And she supposed it didn't matter so long as he followed her instructions so they could get out of here.

"Follow as quietly as you can," she said. "You'll have to lay flat on your stomach and push using your feet and hands, but try to be as gentle on the duct as possible so we don't make much noise."

He grunted. She assumed that was a yes and shimmied into the duct. She had some wiggle room, enough she could turn back to make sure he was behind her. But he filled out the entire rectangular space, his shoulders brushing the metal walls.

Good thing he wasn't claustrophobic. She had a twinge of it just looking at how little space he had in here.

She led the way, slowly and carefully to keep from drawing attention to movement in the duct should anyone happen to be paying attention. She doubted anyone would be since they assumed their motion sensors were still working. But she was a careful thief, if not an entirely cautious one. If she'd been cautious, she wouldn't have gotten into this mess to begin with.

Fortunately, they only had to shimmy through about twenty meters of duct before they reached their destination. From the very quiet grunt behind her, she assumed the journey was not a comfortable one for Christopher.

At their exit air vent, she paused to study the room below. A storage room for electronic equipment and old filing cabinets. There were some tall metal shelves lining the walls. And a few giant photocopy machines currently taking up the center of the room.

Removing the vent from this angle was a little trickier. It was screwed into the wall from the outside rather than the inside. But no actual locks in here. No motion sensors. No cameras.

Just a very handy window.

She bent some of the metal on the screen, giving herself enough room to reach her hand through, and went to work on the screws with her little screw driver, pulled from yet another pocket. She glanced back at Christopher as she worked. He was frowning at her.

"How many pockets does that vest have?" he murmured.

"So many pockets," she said with happy sigh. "So. Many. Pockets."

When she got the screws undone, she angled the screen around to bring it back inside the duct and set it to one side. Then she poked her head out of the open vent to get a better look at the room. All good. Empty. No sounds from any direction to indicate someone had figured out their prize dragon shifter had been stolen.

Yay, her.

The vent opened over one of the metal shelves, which made climbing down both easier, and potentially noisier. So she took a moment to set up a sound dampening spell before crawling out of the vent feet first and easing down the shelves like a ladder.

By the time she reached the ground and turned around to gesture Christopher down, he was already out. He jumped down from a higher shelf than she would have risked and landed next to her in a crouch. They both held still, listening. And when no alarms sounded, he rose to his full height.

Which felt like it took a long time.

"You afraid of heights?" she asked, still keeping her voice low.

"I can fly. I'd make a piss poor dragon if I was afraid of heights."

She snorted a laugh. "Didn't answer my question, though, did you?"

"I'm not afraid of heights."

"Good. How about scaling buildings along thin ledges? That bother you?"

"You were going to do that with a kid?"

"No. I had a different plan. But that won't work with you." She gestured at him. "You're too big."

She couldn't read the expression that crossed his face—a scowl or a repressed smile or just confusion—so she didn't try.

"This is an adjustment to the original escape plan," she said. "My original plan involved more air ducts and a convenient elevator shaft."

"You were going to take a youngling into an elevator shaft?"

Ah, now she could read his expression. That was definitely a scowl of anger. "I wouldn't have let a youngling get hurt," she said. "The elevator was the easiest way down. But the section of air duct we would have had to go through is too narrow for you. So we're making some adjustments."

"Where does the thin ledge outside the building lead?"

"So many questions." She shook her head. "It leads to a room that we can't access through the air vents, but which is in a part of the building not controlled by the group who stole you, and so is an easier room from which to sneak out to a stairwell." She raised a hand. "Before you say it, I've taken care of the cameras and everything inside the stairwell as well. This isn't my first rodeo. But we can't reach the stairwell easily without moving outside the building for a bit."

"Why did you fix the cameras inside the stairwell when you intended on taking the elevator shaft?"

"Because I'm a careful thief who plans for multiple contingencies," she said, hands on her hips. "Are you finished and can we go now? They will notice you're missing sooner rather than later. And that is a complication I'd rather not deal with."

"Have you planned for it?" He sounded smug, like he'd issued a gotcha.

"Of course, I have." She shrugged. "It's just… not a great plan. Better not to have to use it." Also, she'd planned on discovery while moving a child through the building. The fact that Christopher was not, in fact, a child, had really limited her alternative options. "Let's go."

She stalked to the window, trying to ignore the very large dragon shifter at her back. She supposed once she opened the window, he might be able to just shift and fly home. Except they were in the middle of New York City and someone was bound to notice the flying dragon before he could cloak his presence. The dragons weren't exactly a secret, but one flying through the New York skyline would be noticed. And might alert the kidnappers to his absence too soon. The king had wanted his son freed without the kidnappers realizing he was gone.

Also she wasn't sure how fast a dragon shifter could shift. If it wasn't instantaneous, he might just hit the ground before he achieved flight.

That idea gave her a shiver.

"You okay?" Christopher asked.

The question surprised her. "Yes. Why?"

"You shivered. Are you afraid of heights?"

He'd been paying enough attention to notice her shiver. She wasn't sure what to make of that. "I'm not afraid of heights." She grinned. "Actually, I love heights." And tall men. But that wasn't the point. "Scaling heights is second nature to me."

Which was true. She'd been climbing around where she shouldn't have climbed since she was a kid. The magic that made her so good at thieving also seemed to have given her a slight adrenaline addiction.

She studied the window. It wasn't one of the usual sealed ones most high-rise office buildings had these days. This was one of the old school ones that pushed up and could be tipped inside for cleaning. There was a screen over it. And it was locked shut. But neither the screen, nor the lock, were much of a deterrent to her.

Pushing the window up without making noise was actually the hardest part. She used a little "grease" magic to quiet the initial squeak, though that initial sound made her wince and Christopher hiss.

The hiss was an interesting sound. A sound that was very *not* human. And reminded her of his father's court. There'd been a lot of very quiet hissing. Only a handful of dragon shifters had been there, so it wasn't like she'd been surrounded by hundreds of them. Less than half a dozen. But when they're dragon shifters, that's enough.

One is enough.

The one at her back waiting on her to inspect the ledge outside the window was more than enough.

She pulled back inside. "Big enough for me. You'll fit but I hope you have cat-like balance." She asked that last as much as stated it.

He grunted.

A real non-answer answer. Have to do. They didn't have time to argue.

"We're going to the left. We're walking around a corner. And then there will be another window like this one." She didn't mention the other window was a more traditional high-rise window that didn't open. She had that covered and they didn't have time for his questions. "Ready?"

Another grunt.

"Alrighty."

She slid out the window.

FOUR

Myra mostly ignored the drop and the view as she moved out onto the ledge outside the high-rise window. She liked adrenaline, but she also knew how to measure it out so she didn't get shaky. Staring down at the street when she was sneaking out someone who's skills in ledge-walking were in question was a good way to overjump her adrenaline with fear. Wouldn't help anybody with that sort of spike.

If she was alone, she might have enjoyed the view up here. The streets of Manhattan below. The closely packed collection of high-rises. All glass and steel and stone and mostly dark windows rising around her as shadows against the nighttime. The glow of soft pink streetlamps far below. The star-like pattern of occasional window lights scattered over the horizon. The clouds overhead brightened to near orange by the city lights.

This part of Manhattan was mainly business buildings with only the occasional residential place. So at two in the morning, it was quieter than some might think for a supposedly twenty-four-seven city. There was still the occasional bump of cars below, and the releasing air of a bus stopping and opening its door. The cold burn of metal, cement, and tar from a nearby construction sight lingered in the breeze that cooled her cheeks. And a heady punch of salty Hudson River stench caught the very edges of the night air.

Yeah, if she wasn't worried about the very large dragon shifter stepping out onto the very thin ledge next to her, she'd have really enjoyed this view.

Fortunately for them both, this building was one of the old ones with beautiful stone architecture and lovely designs that included things like ledges and decorative carved stone accents. Across the street was one of those smooth steel buildings with nothing but windows and a slick drop to the streets below to recommend it.

She secretly hated the new constructions but not because they made breaking and entering from outside the building harder—she didn't mind that. She had her ways of dealing with that, and she liked the challenge. She just didn't like the aesthetics as much as the stonework and uniqueness of these older buildings.

She inched along the ledge, sliding her feet to ensure she pushed away any potential obstacles that could trip them up, keeping her gaze on their path and destination.

"You doing okay?" she asked, without looking back at him. She took his slightly louder grunt as an "okay."

Adult shifter, used to flying, she reminded herself. This wasn't sending him into a panic. She hoped it wasn't. Fact he was still behind her was a good sign. She hoped.

Going around the building corner was a bit tricky because of one of those decorative stone curlicues she loved so much sticking out just a little far. She showed him what to do by turning so she gripped the stone, her stomach to the decorative swish, and inched around it while holding onto it. She risked a look at him long enough to see he was following her lead. On the other side, she was able to turn again so her back was to the large gray bricks once more. She waited to make sure he managed the maneuver, and when he did without issue, she let out a long breath.

Yeah, she hadn't needed to worry. Apparently, dragons did have cat-like balance.

The window that was their target was two more down. When she reached it, she used the lip over the top of the window for balance as she pulled out yet another tool from her vest pockets. This one a cutting tool. But not just any cutting tool. This one had a little magic in it so the cutting was easy, silent, and the glass wouldn't break.

She stuck the central part of the tool to the window by a suction cup, then stretched out the wire with the cutting tip at the edge and slid the sharp blade around the dark tinted glass. She cut a bigger circle than she normally would to accommodate the large man with her, then slipped the circular chunk now attacked to her cutting tool through the window, setting it down gently on the carpet inside. She slid the rest of the way through the hole, going head first and rolling to get back to her feet. Before Christopher could slip through, she scurried back to move the circle of glass out of his way. She needed that to fix the window and she didn't want the piece cracked.

Christopher came through the hole head first, too. Slithering inside, rather than rolling over his head and back to his feet, as she had. He just crawled inside, down the uncut part of the window and onto the ground like crawling around on all fours was natural. He stood as gracefully as he'd slipped inside, rising to his full height like he did this kind of thing all the time.

Okay. She was impressed.

"Good job," she murmured.

He scowled.

Fair enough. "Sorry for the slight condescension. Wasn't intended."

Another grunt.

"Not a big talker, are you?" she said as she lifted the circle of tinted glass, using the suction cup stuck to the center as a handle. Carefully, she settled the circle back into the hole she'd created, and keeping it in place with one hand on the suction cup, she used her other hand, which she no longer needed for balance on the window sill, to slide the cutting tool at the end of the wire backward over the cut, sealing it this time with some handy magic.

When she stepped back and detached the suction cup, winding the tool back into a small ball she could return to a vest pocket, she admired her handy work. No visible signs of the cut. Even the tinting had smoothed back together without leaving any telltale lines.

"I'm impressed," Christopher said, sounding surprised.

"He speaks!"

She ignored his scowl to examine their surroundings.

There was a large conference table in the middle of the room, with three rectangular shaped gadgets in the center used for, she assumed, audio-visual presentations or whatnot. The table was surrounded by tall-backed swivel chairs. One wall had a screen pulled down. And there was a small cart against the wall, the purpose of which she had no idea, though the faint stale coffee smell made her think a place for setting up coffee service during meetings. Fortunately, this wasn't one of those conference rooms with an entire wall made of glass. And the door was closed.

This was part of a law firm, one of the few other businesses on this floor, and as far as Myra had been able to tell, the firm had no connections with the group that had kidnapped Christopher. Though, the group who'd had the hutzpah to steal a dragon could have hidden their links to the law firm, she supposed. She'd managed to dig pretty deep into the law firm's computer files, though, and there didn't seem to be any ties.

She motioned toward the closed door. "There's a short hallway beyond that and a door just to the left that leads to a set of stairs. There's an alarm on the door. Do not open it. Let me do that." She lowered her chin to give him a look.

His expression never changed.

She assumed that meant he'd listen to her and continued. "We're only going down six flights. Then we'll come back out into the building and take another set of stairs."

"In case they follow our scent?"

"Your scent. Yes." Hers was still disguised by her handy spell.

"Why not go up?"

"Because this is a high-rise, and I don't have a handy way to get us to the next building for an escape."

"I have wings."

"Yes. I'm aware." When he continued to just stare at her, she shook her head and said, "No flying. Too much chance of being spotted. The point is to get out without being spotted. Your dad prefers knowledge of this whole mess doesn't get out of immediate dragon circles."

She reached for the doorknob, but stopped, hand on the knob, her instincts making the hair on the back of her neck stand up.

She lifted her free hand for silence, but Christopher had gone still the minute she did. They both stared at the door. Then she set her ear to the wood. She didn't have shapeshifter hearing or anything. But she did have a little eavesdropping spell. Which she used on the door.

Inside the office, not at the door yet, but still… Someone inside the law firm. Moving around, pushing things that bumped over carpeted floors. A whispered curse.

"Check all the closed rooms," someone said.

She met Christopher's gaze. "Change of plan," she mouthed.

She sent a locking spell through the doorknob. Then scanned the conference room again. Another air duct.

This one was smaller.

She hurried to the side of the room under the duct and whispered, "Boost me up."

She didn't have time to mess around with wall climbing pods or ladders or even the rolling conference room chairs—though that's what she'd have used if she was alone or had an actual child with her. Instead, she had a very large dragon. Strong enough to give her a lift.

The ceiling here wasn't nearly as high as it had been in the room where the kidnappers had kept Christopher. He lifted her—with an ease she'd have to ponder later—and set her up onto his shoulders, which put her at eye level with the duct screen.

No alarms here—she touched the screen to make sure—so she simply had to unscrew the bolts. There was room for her, but barely enough room for him to squeeze in.

Gonna be tight. "Set me down. You first. If you can't fit, we'll have to go back out the window."

Which she didn't want to do because hanging out on a thin ledge when people were looking out windows for you was a lot more precarious than hiding in a vent. Vents had other exits. The only place to run on a building ledge was…off.

Again, with a shocking ease, he lifted her off his shoulders and set her on the ground. Then he boosted himself up to the vent, his arm muscles flexing under his much-damaged shirt. And wasn't that just rude since they didn't have time for her to admire all those lovely muscles at the moment.

To her surprise, he slipped through the opening easier than she would have assumed. Great. So he fit. Now she just had to get up there. But with the lower ceiling, jumping up and grabbing the edge of the duct was within her skill set. She lifted herself into the vent, head first, her feet finding purchase against the smooth wall as she clambered inside.

The vent wasn't large enough for him to turn and face her, so she was looking at his bare feet and his just-barely-angled head so he could see her. She could move enough to get the screen back in place, but she had to use a little magic to hold it up since bolting it back into the wall wasn't an option in such a small, cramped area.

Once she had their trail covered, she motioned him to move. He slid forward on this stomach, pushing against the steel duct with his feet, and managed to move through the narrow space a lot easier and faster than she would have expected. She scrambled after him, going over her mental layout of the building, looking for a good escape option.

They were about to turn a corner in the vent system when she heard a sound from the conference room behind them. She set her hand to Christopher's ankle to stop him. He froze. She did too, her ears straining to hear more than murmurs.

"…telling you they took the stairs."

"Got the cameras back up in there. No one's…"

"…past the alarms. Can get…"

"Shhh."

"He breathes fire, man. This was a bad idea."

Well, Myra thought, at least someone recognized that. Stealing a dragon was a piss poor idea, no matter what they had intended.

She was going to conveniently ignore the fact

that she was *also* stealing a dragon. This was entirely different. The dragon in question was cooperating with her theft.

Knowing they'd figured out her hacks and gotten the security systems turned back on was irritating. How the hell did they find those so fast? Also meant they not only knew Christopher was missing already, they'd have the entire building monitored and maybe even locked down while they hunted for him.

She didn't *think* they could lock down the entire building. Too many other people here. Other businesses. Even if it was two in the morning. But the kidnappers could make getting out without being spotted impossible.

Damn it. So much for getting Christopher away before they knew he was missing.

She wasn't sure how they'd managed it, but she was mightily annoyed they had.

FIVE

Myra held still as she listened to the people in the conference room moving around and shoving at things and then the room grew silent. She held perfectly still for another five minutes. Making sure they hadn't just gone quiet to listen for noise. Even the most patient of people eventually gave in and made sound when they were listening out for a possible thief. So she'd just learned how to outlast most people.

Though, she also had not always been this patient.

Fortunately, Christopher didn't make any sound either and he didn't try to rush her. He was so still that if her hand hadn't been on his ankle, she might have thought he'd slithered on ahead in the narrow air duct.

As she grew more certain the people searching for them had left the conference room, she became increasingly more aware that she was still gripping Christopher's leg. His skin wasn't as hot as she'd have expected from a dragon shifter, but warm enough to feel good. She removed her hand from his ankle.

He met her gaze and she nodded, motioning him to move forward around the curve in the duct. The darkness closed around them, then, making it impossible for her to see, but she'd memorized the layout of these ducts and could tell where they were heading—maybe a little of her magic helped with that, too.

This direction led them to a section of wider vents, but also brought them back in the direction of his captors and that wasn't the direction she wanted to go. The stairwell was no longer an option. And the way she'd gotten in—through a service elevator, after taking care of security sensors accessible from outside the building, and then carefully sneaking through gaps in the guards' routine until she was in a position to disable the rest of the security system from the inside—was not an option now since she had

Christopher with her and he was a lot harder to *sneak* around with given his size.

Her disguise magic was good. She might have been able to slip a child-sized person past the guards and into an elevator. Maybe. A child-sized person she could hold close enough to encompass them with the magic that kept her hidden. But a person as large as Christopher, even held close, was…

Yeah, that wasn't going to work.

When they reached an intersection of vents going in a few different directions, she stopped Christopher with a hand on his ankle again. She was sure no one would see the tell-tale light now, as they were deep enough in the ducts it shouldn't travel, so she cracked one of the thin light tubes she had in an inner pocket of her vest and wrapped it through a fabric tab near her collar. The green glow was enough to allow them to finally see, but not enough to attract attention. The bigger ducts meant they now had enough room they could move around to face each other better, too.

They needed to talk.

"Okay, so," she said, keeping her voice at a whisper. "We need to decide what we do next."

She leaned close enough she was speaking into his ear. Sound carried in vents, farther than light, and she wanted to minimize that. But leaning in so close to him, she was way too aware of his warmth, which was really nice, and also maybe a little too aware of the fact that he hadn't showered in a few days. He still didn't stink as much as she would have expected. He didn't actually *stink* at all. Which was weird. Or maybe she just didn't mind the sweaty smell of him? That was even weirder. She'd write it off to him being a shifter and leave it at that. No reason to investigate why she might sort of half like the smell of him all sweaty.

She blinked hard a few times and said against his ear, "They've blocked the next two options I had for getting us out. Stairwell security is back on. And if that's on, then their elevator security is back on."

"How did you get in?" he asked, also moving so he was speaking against her ear to keep his voice low.

His breath was very warm, too. "Service elevator, disabled security for that from outside. If they found the internal hacking, they found the external hacking."

"So the air ducts?" He looked around, his scowl fierce.

That expression should probably have scared her. He could breathe fire and he looked really really pissed. She wasn't particularly scared. That was probably a character flaw of some kind. Chalk up another one.

"Probably back to being monitored closer to their section of the floor," she said. "They didn't have the entire story rigged, though. Too hard to do with the other businesses. But if we keep going that way—" she nodded to one of the branching ducts, "—we'll crawl right back into their motion sensors. We go that way—" another nod toward a different branching duct, "—we go in a little circle that dead ends back at the law offices and the conference room."

The fact that the people after them had gotten into one of the other businesses to look for them was…worrying. She'd been relying on them not wanting to draw attention by breaking and entering on those other businesses.

"There's a vertical duct that way—" she motioned with her hand down the third directional option they had, "—one that connects multiple floors and runs alongside the elevator bank."

"But?"

"It's made of sheer, slick metal walls and a forty story drop to the ground floor."

"No ladders?"

"No ladders."

"Don't suppose you have something handy for forty stories of climbing in that vest of yours?"

She smiled. "I actually do have something in my vest that can help with a vertical climb."

"That vest is…impressive."

"So is the person who packed the pockets," she said, waggling her eyebrows.

"Yes," he said, a very faint smile cracking his scowl. "Very impressive."

She snorted, and turned away so he wouldn't see how much she wanted to preen under that compliment. "So the problem is," she said when she felt she could whisper in his ear without getting weird about it, "while we won't have to worry about motion sensors in the vertical vent—old building, no one thought about installing them yet—we do have to worry about sound carrying. That shaft connects to the vents on each floor and the way sound carries, we might attract some attention. Any attention risks attracting the attention of the people after you."

"So…we just don't talk?"

She rolled her eyes. "Can you climb down forty stories using rubber hand holds like rock climbing and not grunt or make noise? That's what I'm asking you."

"Yes."

"Good. Because you're going to have to do that."

"This wasn't an option if I was an actual youngling, was it?"

"No."

It had been on her contingency plan, of course. Which was why she knew it was an option at all. But she had really really not wanted to have to use this option with a kid. First time all night she was more grateful than irritated that Christopher wasn't a kid.

Progress or not? She wasn't sure.

Because they didn't have time to fart around, she motioned him down the direction to the vertical air shaft. She conveniently didn't mention that she only had enough of her handy climbing pods for the distance of a few floors, so she'd have to remove them and place them as they went. She didn't want him to worry unnecessarily.

They'd have time for that when they reached the shaft.

Six

Myra looked down the length of the dark, smooth metal shaft, letting the movement of air cool her face. Sound seemed larger and more echoey here, even without her and Christopher making any noise. The space felt open after the ducts, but also… deep. Very very deep.

Deep enough the bottom was shroud in the darkness.

She wasn't afraid of the height, or the climb down. She'd done this a lot—not air shaft climbing, though she had done that, but rock climbing up and down very large, flat mountain faces because it kept her in good shape and kept her climbing skills sharp for just such an occasion. So she wasn't afraid to go down this shaft.

On her own.

Having the son of the dragon king with her, on the other hand…

"Sure you can do this?" she murmured near his ear as she cracked another light tube and tied it to her vest so they'd have a way to see as they climbed down the dark shaft. The old one had faded to a barely-there green glow.

Christopher nodded. "Dragons can climb, you know?"

"I did not know that. Why would a being that can fly need to learn how to climb?"

"Wings are big and get in the way in some spaces. We don't use them all the time." He glanced at her, and his usual scowl softened into something *almost* like a smile. "How much do you know about dragon shifters?"

"Lot less than I thought I did," she said without hesitation.

Like that fact that even having gone without a shower for at least a week, his sweat still didn't smell horrible. After being close to him this long, she was kind of used to it, and might even not mind it.

When she started wondering what he'd smell like after a shower—or maybe in a shower—she blinked hard a few times and said, "Let's go."

She pulled out some of her climbing pods and

leaned into the air shaft to place the first few on the wall. She startled a little when she felt Christopher catch hold of the back of her vest, holding it as she leaned farther down.

She grinned up at him over her shoulder. "'Fraid I'll fall and leave you stranded?" she mostly mouthed since she didn't want to make much sound.

He grunted a reply. Which was just as well. Silence right. They wanted silence.

But it was hard to ignore the little flutter in her stomach. She was supposed to be here getting him out, and here he was making sure she didn't plummet to her death. To be fair, his actions were probably more pragmatic than altruistic or even gallant since she had the vest with all the good stuff in the pockets. Still, it was nice to know he didn't want her to fall and die.

With his hold securing her, she stretched even farther into the shaft and placed an extra few climbing grips to give them a little more room. Then she pushed back inside the vent, or rather she started to push back into the vent and then Christopher just lifted her with an easy, one-handed tug.

Impressive. Little scary. Also a little sexy.

She silently cleared her throat. Then next to his ear, said, "I'm going first, so I can place the pods as I go down. The ones above you that you no longer need? I'm going to have to…call those down to me. I only have enough for about thirty feet."

"You need me to remove them and hand them to you as we go?" he asked, also against her ear.

She enjoyed the warm brush of his breath, which did not smell like sulfur and that was probably very good because they didn't need him breathing fire right now. Though she almost laughed as an image came to mind of a scene from the movie *Die Hard* of fire roaring up an elevator shaft. If there'd been a dragon behind that fire instead of a C4 explosion, she and Christopher could reproduce that scene.

Not that they had time for that.

"Not necessary," she said, answering his question. She wiggled her fingers. "Magic. I've got this. But don't panic when you start seeing the way back up the shaft disappearing? And remember, absolute silence. Grunt in your head."

When she pulled away from him to look him in the eyes, he was back to frowning. But he did nod. So she assumed he'd be good with all this and swung her legs out into the shaft. Smiling a little when he blinked suddenly and reached for her, only checking himself with his hand almost on her vest.

Decent reaction time. Not as good as hers. But decent. And she'd just learned her reaction time could beat a dragon shifter's. That was handy. Especially when she returned to his father's lair and had to deal with him again.

She started down the shaft, falling into the rhythm of climbing easily. She paused far enough down to give him room, then looked up to watch him move out of the shaft and take his first tentative step onto one of the climbing grips. She wanted to tell him not to worry, they'd take his weight—even his substantial weight—because magic. But since they weren't even supposed to be grunting now, she kept her mouth closed and waited.

After his first few, testing steps onto the climbing pods, when they held his weight, he moved fully down into the shaft, climbing a lot easier than she'd feared. She let out a long, silent breath and started climbing again.

She paused when she needed to, to place more grips. And when she got low on the ones in her vest, she stopped long enough to mouth a return spell. The grips above vanished and reappeared in her pocket.

The first time she did this, Christopher looked down at her with his brows raised and eyes wide. It was the first time she noticed his pupils were huge, almost encompassing his irises and making his blue eyes look black. She'd bet cash money he could see in the dark shaft better than she could. Lucky. The green glow from her light tube only traveled so far. The bottom of the shaft was cloaked in darkness and still felt very far beneath them.

It occurred to her that dragons probably did need good night vision, given so many of them liked caves. Even the shifters liked having a "cave" somewhere to hoard things. And dragons of all shapes and sizes were super protective of their hoards, which she'd learned the hard way. So she probably shouldn't have been even a little surprised by good night vision.

She really didn't know nearly as much about dragon shifters as she probably should have before getting on his father's bad side.

Live and learn.

As they passed another air duct feeding back into the building three floors below where they'd entered the shaft, she started to breathe easier. The farther down they went, the closer to escape. Even if they had to leave the shaft before reaching the ground level, it would be a lot easier to escape the building from one of the lower floors without anyone noticing.

So long as their escape plan wasn't discovered *this* time, they were home free.

Cockiness. Her Achille's heel.

When the first flash of blue lightning zipped past her, she cursed that cockiness.

She should have known better.

Seven

Another sizzle of blue lightning flashed into the dark shaft as Myra flattened herself against the wall, trying to make less of a target. She looked up, in the direction the magic shots were coming from, but couldn't see around Christopher.

"Who?" she hissed.

"The kidnappers."

"Shooting magic?"

"Have a wizard with them."

Great.

The dragon king hadn't mentioned a wizard. The possibility of there being shifters among the kidnappers, yes—though he hadn't specified what kind of shifter—but he had absolutely not mentioned a magic wielding wizard. And he really should have mentioned a magic wielding wizard!

No wonder they'd found her security hacks so quickly.

Another zing of electricity arrowed down the shaft, making a mockery of her little green tube light. She squinted against the glare, and said, "Down. Next duct."

They were still ten feet above the duct beneath them, but going back up to a closer duct seemed like a bad idea when that was the direction the dangerous magic was coming from. So down it was.

She heard some shouting and a howl, which was interesting, and there was a lot of cursing—some of which came from her. She set and called the climbing grips as fast as she could while still moving downward as fast as she could go. Blue magic ricocheted off the smooth metal walls inside the shaft. Her heartbeat pounded hard.

A grunt from just above her.

She looked up in time to see Christopher leaning awkwardly back, his hands slipping from the climbing grip.

"No!"

She grabbed his hand on the way past, clutching his forearm as he wrapped his fingers around hers. His skin was slick with sweat, and he weighed a ton. Not good for her hold. She squeezed tight to his hand and held her body against the wall to aid her grip on the climbing pod. And because she needed it, she added a little magic to keep her own fingers from slipping.

"Let me go," Christopher said. "I'm too heavy. You'll fall."

"Shut. Up. Let me concentrate."

She glanced up again. Now she could see the wizard leaning out of the air vent three floors up. His features were hard to see from this distance, though she suspected if she'd been a shifter of some kind, she would have made out more than the dark hair and vaguely pale skin. Even the *he* part of her assessment might be wrong. Didn't matter. The wizard fired more blue lightning down into the shaft, this time aiming at the wall opposite, angling the shot like a ball on a pool table, trying to hit them on the ricochet.

"That's cheating!" she shouted up at the wizard.

There were more howls behind him and then another head poked out of the vent.

"Thirty-fourth floor," the head said. "Go. Get them."

"Let me go," Christopher said again.

She was straining to hold him and not lose her grip, hard enough when he was holding onto her.

When she felt his hand loosening, she cursed. "Stop that! I'm not letting you fall."

But she couldn't climb like this. And the duct opening was still too far below. And they were going to have company there soon.

"I'm placing more grips. Get ready." She hated doing this purely with magic because she couldn't ensure they were secure setting them this way. But beggars couldn't be choosers.

She narrowed her eyes to concentrate and focused on moving the climbing pods around, sending all the ones left above her to a ragged ladder like line below her.

"Take hold of one." She grunted when she felt Christopher gain purchase, easing some of his weight from her. "Make sure it holds before you let go of me."

"Got it," he said, releasing her arm.

She looked down and let out a breath, seeing him once again holding onto the grips. "Down to the vent," she ordered, then looked up again.

In time to see a blue sizzle of lightning arrowing right for her. "Shit." She flattened against the wall, moving as far to one side as she could while still holding the pods.

Wasn't far enough. The magic shot hit her arm, sending a shockwave of electrical pain through her limb.

Her body jolted. Her fingers loosened. Her vision darkened.

She let out a pissed off gasp when her body didn't respond. Her stomach tumbled, but even that felt distant and out of her control. She couldn't scramble to regain her hold. She couldn't even curse. She couldn't do anything.

But fall down the nearly forty story air shaft.

The last thing she saw before the darkness swallowed her was Christopher, hand outstretched, reaching for her.

EIGHT

Myra snapped awake, suddenly, but held herself perfectly still as she scrambled to remember why she'd been unconscious. Cold wind hit her face before she even had her eyes open. Looking down, she blinked. The cityscape of high-rise buildings rolling past *below* her was…unexpected.

Without looking away from those passing buildings, she murmured, "This is going to require some explanation."

"Soon," Christopher said from above her.

The feel of arms around her back and under her legs, the air so cold and wind so sharp it made her eyes water, the heat pumping off the body she was cradled against. A lot of disorienting sensations hitting her all at once. Including the height. She wasn't afraid of heights. Normally. But usually, she had some sort of control on just how high she was.

She forced herself to look up. Christopher's face, still in human form above her, his gaze out over the city, his eyes glowing a little in the darkness. The very large wings sprouting from his back and shoulders were new.

He'd had a shirt on when she'd broken him out of his cell. The shirt was gone now. Not even scraps to show for it. And his bare skin was a good deal warmer than it had been earlier in the night. That heat kept her from shivering with the cold at this altitude. There was a sweep of purple and yellow scales over his skin now. The color of the scales blended into the wings, which had strong bone ridges with a thin purple membrane between bones. They reminded her of a bat's wings. Except the wing span was easily…twenty, thirty feet. Hard to tell from her angle dangling in his arms under him. Like a fish in a hawk's talons. Except this hawk was a lot bigger. And his talons were holding her in a warm, comfortable cocoon.

And she was pretty sure Christopher didn't intend on devouring her. In the bad way.

"I'm not splat at the bottom of an air shaft," she said. And though her voice seemed to whip away from her on the cold air, he apparently heard her just fine because he answered.

"No."

"You can do partial shifts?"

"I can do partial shifts."

Handy. "The wizard and the others?"

She'd swear he winced. But it was hard to tell at this angle and with the overall fact that they were flying and he was concentrating on that.

"I might have left some…crisped shifters and a very crisped wizard in the air ducts after I saved you."

She nodded. Skipping right past the part where he'd saved her—she was probably going to need solid ground under her for that one—she said, "That's going to stink up the place. Imagine the maintenance crew are going to be a little surprised when they discover what's causing the smell."

His mouth ticked up in an almost-smile. It was a nice almost-smile.

She was very tempted to kiss that mouth, and that almost-smile. But she didn't want to distract or startle him while he was flying.

He dipped his wings to one side, picking up a new air current, and banked to the left toward one of the tallest buildings around. Fascinated as she was by the sight of him, she turned away to assess where they were. Everything looked different from this angle, of course, but she was pretty sure they were somewhere in Midtown, higher end, getting close to the Park. Since it was the middle of the night and the park would be empty but for the unsavory types, she wondered if that's where they were heading. What did a dragon shifter care about unsavory human types, right?

But no, the tall building seemed to be his target.

Another of the older buildings, with excellent stonework, a mix of red brick and white stone balconies and accents. This one had a flat roof, with the usual old water tower, lines of air vents, and a raised building where a stairwell would be. The edge around the roof was about waist high with lovely carved crenellated details. Landing on that roof in the arms of a dragon when those kinds of details reminded her of castles was as interesting as waking up high in the air with the city racing past below.

Interesting seemed to be her go-to word tonight.

She was trying to decide if she liked interesting or not when Christopher touched down on the roof. She normally did like interesting. Usually interesting meant fun. Glancing up at Christopher as he continued to hold her in his arms and stare down at her, she thought this might just be fun. She also thought his expression was fascinating. And she was very tempted to touch his jaw and see how he reacted.

Then she frowned. "How old are you, really? In dragon terms." She raised her eyebrows. "Like, if I were to kiss you, would that be some sort of… child molestation?" The idea horrified her.

His expression turned into a scowl. "No. Of course not. I'm not *that* young." His scowl softened, but his frown didn't go away. "You really don't know much about dragon shifters, do you?"

"Nope." She shrugged and started to pat his chest so he'd set her down, but the feel of warm muscles and solid shoulders momentarily distracted her. So she let her hands linger on his scale-covered skin, the texture smooth and warm. And because she was watching, she saw his eyes whirl from nearly black with a golden glow over them to something with a more purple glow. None of it like his blue eyes from earlier that night, but fascinating to watch.

"So…" she murmured. "Age-wise for a dragon?"

"Old enough," he said, his voice deeper now and his gaze more intent.

Her stomach tingled and tightened at that, a

little tremor of excitement running through her. And again she thought the word *interesting*.

With a great deal of reluctance, she patted his shoulders and said, "Better set me down before you get tired."

Not that he showed any signs of that. He seemed to hold her like she weighed little and could do this all night. Which was a thought one step farther than her brain could handle at that moment.

He did slowly release her legs so she dropped to the ground, but he kept an arm around her as she got her balance. For which she was grateful, because the wobbly feeling she got standing on her own caught her off guard.

"So, what happened?" She vaguely remembered getting hit by the wizard bolt, and the sensation of helplessly falling would stick with her for years. But then the blackness and… And that was it.

"The wizard was tossing around magic designed to render us unconscious, and they didn't care if you fell and died."

"Would you have died if you fell?" she asked.

"Not died. Just been wounded."

Still. "Glad none of that happened." She nodded to his wings. "You shifted in the air shaft?" His wings actually looked too big for the space they'd been in, so… "How did that work?"

"I can adjust the size of my wings," he said.

That earned him an eyebrow raise. "Wow. Might have been useful to know that earlier in the night."

"You didn't want me to shift."

She gave him a look.

"How did you end up working for my father if you know so little about dragon shifters?"

She waved a hand in the air. "Lost a stupid bet. Long story."

"We have time now."

She sighed. This was embarrassing. "The short explanation is that I assumed when I broke into your father's hoard, I'd just steal the least valuable thing there was. No one would miss it. I'd get out and win my bet. No harm no foul. Except, I sort of underestimated how pissed your dad would be just by me getting into the hoard."

"Because no one should have gotten anywhere near his hoard," Christopher said, sounding both aghast and, she thought, maybe a little impressed. "Were you supposed to steal something in particular? Who hired you?"

His sudden intensity on those last two questions had her raising her hands, a defensive gesture. "First, no one hires me. Most of the time.

I steal for myself. Not for other people. And I don't steal from people who would miss what I took. In fact, most of the people I steal from have so much stuff, they've forgotten most of it exists. Do you know how much *stuff* people collect?"

"I'm a dragon. I have an idea."

She both winced and smiled at that. "Your dad's hoard was pretty impressive." At his look, she said, "I wasn't there for anything in particular. Just a trinket to prove I'd managed to get in. It was a bet. A dare with financial backing, if you will. Old rival. We're always testing each other. I figured this one was easy money." She shrugged. "Who knew?"

"Anyone who knows anything about dragon shifters would have known."

"We've already established I don't know nearly as much as I should have." And really, she needed to rectify that situation. Or never deal with dragon shifters again. Either way.

Except, as she looked up at Christopher, with his magnificent wings folded against his back, and that very interesting purple glow in his eyes, and his warm, solid shoulders, she knew she didn't want to stop dealing with *all* dragon shifters.

He crossed his arms, a gesture that emphasized his shoulders and chest muscles. She narrowed her eyes. Had he done that on purpose? He'd done that on purpose.

Then he spoke and she changed her mind about his motivation for crossing his arms.

"The shifters and wizard who kidnapped me? They wanted something from my father's hoard."

Shit. "I…didn't know that. Was that why your father was so pissed?"

"My father would always be pissed about someone breaking into his hoard. It's supposed to be impossible."

"Compliment? No? Okay, so… What did the shifters and wizard want? And what kind of shifters were these? Your father failed to mention the species." And the wizard. But she wasn't going to get into that part now.

Christopher skipped over the species question, too. "My father has a magical artifact in his hoard that could turn shifters into indestructible monsters."

"That sounds bad."

"Which is why my father keeps it secured in his hoard where it's supposed to be safe from thieves."

"Oops?" She wasn't sure what to say to that. Breaking into the hoard had been challenging, but not impossible. At least not for someone like her.

And frankly, she was a little proud of that. Even if it had gotten her into some trouble.

"The shifters couldn't find anyone to break in, no one capable of it anyway. They hired the wizard to help. He failed."

She wanted to wince again, but also wanted to preen.

"Did this rival of yours ask you to bring out something specific?"

"Nope. Nothing. Just something to prove I'd been there." But she was starting to see why this all looked very suspicious. "Why did your father send me to steal you back rather than kill me? He had to think I was part of all this."

"You weren't?"

"Of course not." She put her hands on her hips and glared at him. "I told you already, I wasn't going to steal anything of value or even anything specific. A coin or something would have done."

"But it could have just been a test run. Your rival setting you up to steal something larger for them later?"

She let her arms drop as she considered that. Damn it. "Possible. He's a real asshole. That wouldn't be beyond his machinations." Made her feel stupid for falling for the trick, though. She was going to have to repay that asshole. "Except I'm not a hired thief. I only steal for myself." She shrugged. "Mostly for the challenge. And because I'm good at it." At his look, she said, "What? It's fun."

"Could he have 'bet' you that you couldn't steal something like the artifact? Would you have tried then?"

"No idea." At his scowl, she said, "If I didn't know what the artifact was, how valuable it was, or what it could do, I wouldn't agree until I'd done some research. Does that help?"

"And when you discovered what it could do?"

"You mean when I learned it could magically turn shifters into unkillable monsters, would I still steal it and hand it over to an asshole rival? No. Of course not."

She wanted to be offended that he'd asked. But to be fair, they'd known each other a few hours, and she was here because she'd broken into his father's hoard, and really, she didn't have a lot of moral ground to stand on when it came to thieving. Still. She wasn't the kind of thief to want indestructible shifters loosed on the world. That would be bad for everyone. Thieves included.

Christopher stared at her for a long moment, his arms still crossed, before he finally said, "My father must have seen that strange thread of honesty in you."

"Strange?"

"For a thief."

Okay. She'd give him that.

"Or he wouldn't have sent you to break in and free me."

"I am good at stealing things. Even things that have already been stolen." Which reminded her. "How on earth did they manage to steal you? Being as how you're…" She gestured at him, the sweep of her hands taking in the wings and vaguely referring back to the fact that he'd turned the shifters and wizard in those air ducts into burnt husks.

"Why do you keep referring to what happened to me as me being stolen and not me being kidnapped?"

"I don't deal with kidnappers. I'm a thief. I deal in stolen things."

"Semantics."

"But it works for me. So how did they manage to get to you?"

The faint color on his cheeks, high on those already cut cheekbones, was probably the most charming thing she'd ever seen.

"I was…tricked," he said, turning his head enough he was no longer meeting her gaze.

"Tricked?"

"They set a trap for me." His jaw locked tight on that.

She raised her brows. "Trap?"

"I might have a problem with…"

"With?" Her instincts rose and she stilled. What the hell did a dragon shifter have a problem with that it made him so nervous? Couldn't be anything good.

"I… I can't abide a…" He muttered the last few words so she couldn't hear them.

"A what?" She leaned in closer to hear him better.

"A damsel in distress," he barked out, without meeting her gaze.

She nodded, staring up at him for a long minute. "A dragon. Who worries about…damsels in distress? That's…"

"Interesting?"

"I was thinking more along the lines of ironic and funny, but we can go with interesting here." She felt a smile tugging at her lips and pressed them together so she didn't laugh out loud. "Spotted a woman in trouble. Swooped in to save the day. She was part of a trap. You got clobbered by the wizard's anti-dragon magic."

"Something like that."

"Oh, I have to hear this."

He huffed out a breath and she'd swear there was steam on the huff. He seemed to be radiating a little more heat, too. But it was really the rosy color in his cheeks she found most delightful.

"Mostly…it was like you guessed. She was a shifter, a lion shifter. Not in any danger in the end. And the wizard… They had the containment collar on me before I knew what was happening. Knocked me out. I woke up in the cell."

She nodded, her lips pursed, waiting for him to meet her gaze. He didn't. So she nudged his chin with her fingers. His skin was scorching hot, but it felt weirdly good and that was something she'd think about at some point in the future.

When he finally met her gaze, she said, "That's the sweetest way I've ever heard for someone to get trapped. No reason to be embarrassed."

"It's…not something my dragon brethren understand."

"I imagine. What with eating virgins and all that."

He scowled again and it wiped away some of the mortification in his expression. "That's real dragons. Not dragon shifters. And even real dragons don't always do that. And haven't done that in centuries."

"Told you I don't know much about dragons." She shrugged.

"You don't…" He let out a breath. "You don't think it's a weakness?"

"Not even a little."

"Got me captured by people who wanted to blackmail my father and steal an artifact to create monsters."

"Shit happens."

His charming smile cracked through his scowl. She returned it with a big grin. Bumping his shoulder, which was still really warm, she wandered closer to the edge of the roof, so she could take in the view.

"Pretty risky, you shifting, even partially, to rescue me. You could have let me fall."

"You did just hear what I said about damsels in distress, right?"

She chuckled. "Fine." She eyed the wings on his back, folded tightly over his spine, but the tops rising several feet above his already impressive height. "Still, pretty risking. Flying out over the city like that. Don't care how late it is, someone probably saw you. Your father wanted to keep this all quiet."

"I cloaked—yes, I can do that—but most people wouldn't be expecting to see a partially shifted dragon at this time of night over the city, so even if they did see me, they wouldn't believe what they were seeing?"

"Probably think you were Batman or someone."

"You think my wings look like bat's wings?" He spread them out, puffing up in a way that was supposed to be impressive and succeeded spectacularly.

"Is that insulting to a dragon? I feel like you found that insulting." She laughed and said, "I like your wings."

"Hmm." He gave them a little flutter before folding them in tight to his back again.

She looked out over the dark cityscape, at the surrounding high-rises with their occasional lit windows, the dark shadow of Central Park a few blocks away, the lines of car lights running up and down the square Midtown blocks. The wind was a lot less cold when they weren't flying, but it was still crisp and chilly on the rooftop. A sharp contrast to the heat pumping off the man next to her.

Not just man. Dragon.

So much she didn't know about dragons.

She gave him a look from the side of her eye. "Do you have a hoard? Like your father's."

"If I do, would you steal from it?"

"Nothing you'd miss," she said with a shrug.

His mouth twitched. Then more seriously, "What do you do with the things you steal?"

"If I need the money, I sell my take through a very cooperative auction house that likes the caliber of items I bring them. They don't ask too many questions of me or the purchasers, no one is really stuck on provenance, and we're all happy with the financial outcome of the exchange. If I don't need the money…" Shrug again. "I usually return whatever I stole the next night, or the next week."

He blinked down at her. "You return stuff you've stolen?"

"Sometimes. Depends. Why?"

"That's…"

She smiled. "Interesting?"

"That's a good word for it."

She nodded, her gaze skimming the skyscrapers, and the spectacular view of Manhattan from this height. "It is my go-to word tonight. Interesting."

"Speaking of." He moved just a little closer, his gaze moving over the view like hers. "I seem to recall you saying something about kissing me."

"I did, didn't I?" She swallowed.

"You never did, though. Kiss me, I mean. Even though I'm old enough."

Her cheeks heated at the reminder of her worry. "I never did. I wasn't sure… I thought you might object."

"I wouldn't object."

She glanced up at him just as he glanced down at her. "Interesting," she murmured.

He smiled. A smile that sent a lot of trembly sparks through her body. A smile she could really get used to.

They leaned in at the same time. Meeting in the middle. Her going up on her toes. Him leaning over, a hand on the low wall circling the roof. His lips were incredibly soft. The kiss was very gentle. And her insides danced in such anticipation, she melted closer.

"Interesting," he murmured when he pulled back.

"Mmm." Yeah. The kind of interesting she'd like to indulge in more.

This close to him, she realized his scent was… different now. The flight or maybe the partial shift must have worked like a shower because there was no longer that low-level stress sweat smell. Now he almost smelled like…

"Why do you smell like sugar cookies now?" she asked.

He raised his brows. "Do you like sugar cookies?"

"Love them. But I've never smelled a person who smelled like sugar cookies." It was one of those sweet vanilla scents that made her want to get closer and draw more of it in. Subtle. Not overpowering. But there. Teasing her and making her a little hungry.

His smile did something more to that hunger. A hunger that had nothing to do with food.

"You should probably start to learn more about dragon shifters," he said.

Sounded like a threat and a promise at the same time.

Like a dare.

She was a sucker for a dare.

"Maybe I should." Her gaze dropped to his mouth. To that smile. Then she met his gaze. The purple glow over his blue eyes drew her like a lure. "We should probably let your father know you're out now."

"Probably." He glanced out over the skyline. "Want to fly there?"

She grinned and looked out over the skyline as well. "Sounds…" She gave him a look. "Interesting."

He laughed, the sound making her heart do that fluttery pounding thing. Then he swept her up into his arms so fast she gasped. She wrapped her arms around his neck. Feeling surprisingly secure like this.

"Hold tight," he murmured next to her ear. Then he bent his knees and launched into the sky, his wings snapping open and taking two powerful downbeats before he caught an air current that brought them higher.

Myra laughed even as her stomach dropped to her toes and a thin edge of fear sent adrenaline into her blood. She loved that feeling.

She glanced up at Christopher, just as he smiled down at her.

Yeah. She definitely needed to learn more about dragon shifters.

She had a feeling she was going to be spending a lot more time with one of them.

THANK YOU

Thanks for reading DRAGON THIEF! I hope you enjoyed this introduction to Myra and Christopher. Originally, I wrote this story for the collection WHO STEALS A DRAGON, in which I pose that question at the start of each story and then answer it in six different genres with six different types of dragons. This story was the Paranormal Romance story. And I enjoyed Myra and Christopher so much, I knew I wanted to write more about them.

The Dragon Thief series grew from that. This version of the story is almost identical to what is in WHO STEALS A DRAGON. I've corrected a few copyedit mistakes missed on the first version, and tweaked a few things to fit the world building I've been doing on later stories. But it is, overall, the same as the original story.

From here, Myra and Christopher have a lot more adventures. The next novella in the series is THE CHICAGO JOB, out now.

If you've enjoyed this story and want to read more of my work, you can find all my books at KatSimonsBooks or at my author website. If you'd like to keep up to date on my releases and news, the best place to do that is my newsletter. The newsletter comes out (mostly) monthly, includes all the new releases, news, excerpts, cover reveals, occasional free stories, and I have two exclusive stories available for new subscribers.

Alternatively, you can follow my author page at your favorite vendor or at BookBub. I can also be found lurking and occasionally posting baking pictures at Instagram, Bluesky, and Facebook.

Thanks again for reading!

Kat

Don't miss the next story in the
Dragon Thief series!

THE CHICAGO JOB

Keep Reading for an excerpt.

THE CHICAGO JOB
EXCERPT

ONE

Taking a stupid bet and breaking into the dragon king's hoard had been Myra's first mistake.

Thinking she'd be able to get away with doing just one job to make up for that lapse in judgement had been her second.

She was still deciding if kissing the dragon king's son had been the third mistake. Jury was still out. Depended on how this current confrontation went.

Standing in the middle of the dragon king's court, in an elaborate mansion some people might have called a castle, amidst a compound of other buildings, circled by a fortified wall, built among the hills and hard gray rock in the far upper west end of Manhattan, Myra had assumed she'd hand

Christopher over to his father, bid them both farewell, and that would be her done with the dragons. At least with the king. With Christopher…

Again, jury still out.

But the dragon king had decided to throw all those assumptions into the trash and make Myra rethink all her life choices. Or at least the one, very bad choice that had put pride before common sense when she took that bet.

She suspected the reason the king wasn't done with her yet was because she'd *succeeded* in breeching his hoard more than the fact that she'd attempted it. Lots of thieves eventually attempted to break into a dragon hoard. Hard to resist all that gold and jewelry and cash and bonds and…well, the wealth. The sheer wealth. Who could resist that?

But most thieves couldn't get around the security of a dragon hoard. Especially not a dragon king's hoard. They usually got caught somewhere along that process, still a long way from actually reaching the treasure.

Myra had gotten caught standing in the middle of the hoard admiring some of the crown jewels.

Fortunately for her, those skills were more valuable to the dragon king than killing her as an example would have been. And also fortunately—

maybe?—she'd broken in just after the king's son had gotten stolen. Yes, yes, technically Christopher insisted he'd been kidnapped, not stolen. But she was a thief. She stole things. She thought in terms of theft. Not kidnapping. Returning a stolen item was within her purview.

And that's what she'd done. Retrieved Christopher from the shapeshifters and wizard who'd stolen him, and then returned him to the king unharmed. Mostly.

True, she'd assumed she'd been sent in to rescue a kid—because the king kept calling his son a youngling—and her plan to get back out of the high-rise building had needed to be changed at the last minute. She was good at improvisation, though. And she'd had backup plans. Multiple backup plans.

Those plans just hadn't accounted for the near seven-foot-tall wall of muscle and adult male physique standing next to her.

Still, they'd gotten out alive and unsinged. Only the kidnappers had gotten burned. Myra considered that a job well done.

The king had decided that her completing this excellent bit of work was not quite enough.

"Father, you've asked enough of her. Let it go." Christopher shifted his position to stand just a little in front of her as they faced his father, which was nice because standing before a dragon king was intimidating as hell even if the king was in human and not dragon form at that moment.

Sitting on an elaborate throne made of bones and gold with some winking jewelry in between. She'd eyed that throne the first time she'd seen it, wondering how hard it would be to remove, say, that little diamond near the base without anyone noticing.

She had not been left alone for long enough to find out.

Like his son, the dragon king was a huge man, standing well over six and a half feet tall in human form, with dark black curly hair cut neatly, and light eyes that switched from blue to green depending on the light. His skin tone was pale in this form. She'd never personally seen him in dragon form, but the rumor was his scales were bronze colored, with a bit of red. She had no idea how old he was because dragon shifters aged different to humans, but he'd been around and been king for a long time, so she assumed he was old. There were silver threads in his dark hair, but it was hard to tell if those were natural or an affectation to give himself gravitas. With the king, you just couldn't be sure.

Unlike his son, the king was what one would call classically handsome. The bones on his face and jaw were strong, his features perfectly symmetrical, his forehead high under his crown, his lips thin but suited his facial structure. Had he wanted to, the king could have made a killing as a leading man in Hollywood. Probably wouldn't have even mattered if he could act. Because even outside of the good looks, he was compelling. There was a sort of aura to him that made people notice him. An inner power that took up space and commanded rooms.

He and Christopher shared that trait even if they didn't share much in the way of looks.

Probably helped they could both shift into dragons the size of low-rise buildings.

"She is not done with repaying me for my magnanimous decision not to kill her," the king said in answer to his son, his voice deep, rolling through the high ceiling room like thunder.

"She showed you exactly where your security systems were weak and vulnerable before anyone with real nefarious intent got in," Christopher said. "And she assisted me in breaking out of the tower so you couldn't be forced to do something…difficult to take back."

The shifters and wizard had been trying to get a relic the king kept in his hoard that, according to Christopher, turned shifters into unkillable monsters. That would have been bad. She'd been delighted not to have been the one committing that fuck up and handing the relic over. No one had even mentioned a relic to her. She'd taken a bet from an old rival, to prove she could get into the hoard. And all she'd intended on taking out was a trinket to prove she'd been there.

But, after hearing what Christopher had to say about his kidnappers, she realized she'd been the guinea pig, the one they'd sent in to see if it was even possible to get into the king's hoard. Her rival might have even been working with the shifters, though she'd have to question him to find out. Even if he hadn't, even if he'd been tricked into issuing her the bet, the end result had been her getting into the king's hoard, only to get caught.

Kidnapping Christopher was their insurance plan if the break in hadn't succeeded. Stealing the relic, or blackmailing the king with one of his son's lives…either way would get the job done.

No one expected the king to hire a thief to get Christopher back.

"One more job," the king said. "Nothing that isn't within your realm of expertise." He spoke directly to Myra, ignoring his son's comment. "And we will consider ourselves even."

"My debt was paid when I got Christopher back," she said. "You want me to do a job for you now, that'll require payment. Up front. And details before I accept."

She was bluffing. Big time.

First, she never worked for other people. No one hired her to steal things. She stole because she wanted to. What she wanted to. When she wanted to.

But in reality, if the dragon king told you to do a job for him, there wasn't an awful lot someone like her could do about it. Except turn it down and then die. She didn't want to die, so she'd accept the job. So long as it didn't involve doing something she didn't do. Like kill people.

The king's expression tightened but that was his only show of tension. A blink and he smiled at her. It was not a comforting smile. There were a lot of teeth involved. Reminding her that in his other form, the king could swallow her whole.

"There's a relic that has long eluded me. But it would be infinitely safer inside my hoard rather than loose for any…any unscrupulous individual to access."

"What's this relic do?" She'd been left in the dark about the monster creating relic last time. She didn't want to make that same mistake.

"Nothing humans need worry about."

She came within a microsecond of snort-laughing at that comment. With all the dragons around Manhattan, a human with any sense in their head always worried about the things those dragons did or were interested in. Just common sense in this world. The dragons might go out of their way not to appear as dragons very often. And they usually cloaked when flying around for the comfort and peace of mind of humans. But that didn't keep humans from worrying about what the dragons did.

Instead of laughing, she gave the king a very level look. She couldn't completely ignore the unfortunate tingle of curiosity that moved through her blood, though.

"What's the relic?" she said.

She wasn't saying she'd actually take the job. But she wasn't saying she wouldn't either. In fact, even though working for the dragon king was a bad idea and she didn't consider she owed him anything else anymore—she *had* just brought him back his son alive and well—her own curiosity did tend to get the better of her.

Between her curiosity and her professional pride lay the seeds of her own destruction.

But what could a thief do.

Don't miss the next adventure in
the Dragon Thief series.

THE CHICAGO JOB

Out now!

Join Kat's Newsletter

Stay Up-to-Date

On all Kat's News, Updates, and fun extras

New Subscriber Get Two Exclusive Stories Just for Signing up!

bit.ly/KatSimonsNewsletter

Thanks for Reading!

As a valued reader I'd like to off you a special Dragon Thief discount code to KatSimonsBooks

MYRA10

Enter this code at checkout for a 10% discount off everything in your cart!

Thank you!

One use per customer, good for everything in the store, one time use only.

KATSIMONSBOOKS.COM

The
CARY REDMOND
Series

KAT SIMONS
KAT SIMONS
KAT SIMONS
KAT SIMONS
KAT SIMONS
KAT SIMONS
KAT SIMONS

THE TROUBLE WITH
SHIFTERS AND
FAE
A CARY REDMOND

THE TROUBLE WITH
MAGES AND
FAERIES
A CARY

THE TROUBLE WITH
FATES

THE TROUBLE WITH
LEOPARDS AND SHIFTERS
A CARY R

THE TROUBLE WITH
WARDS AND
ENEMIES
A CARY REDMOND NOVEL

THE TROUBLE WITH
GHOULS AND
SERIAL KILLERS
A CARY REDMOND NOVEL

THE TROUBLE WITH
BLACK CATS
AND DEMONS
A CARY REDMOND NOVEL

GOT TROUBLE?

Don't Miss a Single Book in this
Action-Packed Romantic Urban Fantasy Series

PARANORMAL ROMANCE

From

KAT SIMONS

Books By Kat Simons

Dragon Thief Series

<u>Season One</u>

Dragon Thief

The Chicago Job

The Poisons Book Job

The Vault Job

The Femme Fatale Job

The Scavenger Job

<u>Season Two</u>

The Crown of Kingship Job

The Green Scroll Job

The Payback Job

Pick Your Genre Collections

Who Steals a Dragon

The Cary Redmond Series

* The Trouble Black Cats and Demons * The Trouble with Ghouls and Serial Killers * The Trouble with

Leopard Queens and Shifter Wars * The Trouble with Baby Gods and Vampires * The Trouble with Magic and Faery Curses * The Trouble with Wizards and Old Enemies * The Trouble with Death and Demon Gods

The Cary Redmond Series Box Set Books 1-3

Cary Redmond Short Stories

* When Cary Met Jaxer * When Cary Met Pickles * When Cary Met Marianne * When Cary Met Lucy * When Cary Met Angie * Cary and Deacon (Try to) Go on a Date * Date Night Take Two * Third Date's the Charm * Cary vs the Goblin King * Dinner with the Joneses * Cary and the Cursed Jack-O'-Lantern * Cary and the Demon Witch * Cary Goes to Hawaii * Cary Holidays * Cary and Dragons and Goblins * Cary's Galentine's Day * Cary at the Haunt and Howl * Cary's Leprechaun Troubles * Cary's Beltane Night Out *

When Cary Met the Good Guys (Collection 1)

Dates, Dinners, and Other Disasters (Collection 2)

Witches and Weavers and Ghosts, Oh Boy (Collection 3)

A Very Cary Holiday (Collection 4)

Romancing the Leopard: A Tiger Shifters-Cary Redmond Crossover Novel

Tiger Shifters Series

* Once Upon a Tiger * Along Came a Tiger * Here There Be Tigers * Her Tiger To Take * To Tempt a Tiger * Down Will Come Tiger * To Catch a Tiger * What a Tiger Wants * Taming Her Tiger

Tiger Shifters Series Vol 1 (Books 1 - 3)

Tiger Shifters Series Vol 2 (Books 4 - 6)

Seven Families Series

Wolf Family

Darkness in Stone

Redemption in Stone

Fated in Stone

Wolf in Stone: A Seven Families Box Set, Books 1-3

Demon Witch Series

Howling Dreadful

Moonlit Strange

Bone Lantern Witch

Spiderweb Witch

Storm Shadow Witch

Darkling Mist Witch

Joan of Kerry Series

Joan of Kerry: Joan and the Abhartach

Joan and the Leprechaun

Joan and the Kraken

Joan and the Selkie

Joan and the Goblins

Haunts and Howls Collections

Haunts and Howls and Guardian Spells

Haunts and Howls Where Demons Dwell

Haunts and Howls and Jesters Bells

*Tombstone Wizard * The Unshattered Sword *
Destiny Through the Cats Eyes * Going Out of
Business: Everything's for Sale * Anger Management *
Demonic Dates * Friday's Curious Shop * The Museum
of Small Art's Everyman * Burning Inside a Stone
Circle * Bored Questless * I Just Ate a Bug * Ting Ling
* Sophie Saves the World * Black Water Hawthorns
*To Dance in Fallow Fields at Midnight *

More Books by Kat Simons

Contemporary Romances

Designed for You

Poinsettias and Possibilities

Mystery and Thrillers

Ross and O'Neill Adventures

Galileo's Pendulum

Percy James Mysteries

Movies May Murder

Cookies Can't Crime

Diamonds Do Damage

Replicas Risk Ruin

Vacation Deadly: An Action Adventure Thriller
Collection

ABOUT THE AUTHOR

Kat Simons earned her Ph.D. in animal behavior, working with animals as diverse as dolphins and deer. She brought her experience and knowledge of biology to her paranormal romance and urban fantasy fiction, where she delights in taking nature and turning it on its ear. She writes urban fantasy, contemporary fantasy, and paranormal romance in series which combine action adventure, the otherworldly, and a frequent dose of sexy romance.

The newest book in her bestselling romantic urban fantasy series about Protector Cary Redmond, The Trouble with Shifters and Fae Courts, sees a new direction for the intrepid Protector, her sexy leopard shifter mate, and the entire crew. Kat also launched a new novella length Paranormal Romance series that follows the adventures of a magical thief and the dragon shifter prince she just can't seem to shake—and really doesn't want to. The first season of the Dragon Thief series released throughout 2024.

Season Two begins in 2025 with The Crown of Kingship Job.

For something a little different, Kat also publishes fantasy, science fiction, and the occasional hockey romance under the name Isabo Kelly (https://www.isabokelly.com).

After traveling the world, living in places like Hawaii, Germany, and Ireland, Kat now lives in New York City with her family and a library's worth of books.

For more on Kat and her future books

Website: https://www.katsimons.com/
Newsletter: https://bit.ly/KatSimonsNewsletter

KatSimonsBooks
https://www.katsimonsbooks.com
https://www.TheCafeatKatSimonsBooks.com

Social Media
Facebook Page: https://www.facebook.com/
KatSimonsAuthor
BookBub: https://www.bookbub.com/authors/kat-
simons
Bluesky: https://bsky.app/profile/katsimons.bsky.
social
Instagram: https://www.instagram.com/isabokelly/
Threads: https://www.threads.net/@isabokelly

www.ingramcontent.com/pod-product-compliance
Lightning Source LLC
Chambersburg PA
CBHW030903200726
48289CB00003B/879